Beautiful Shades of Love

ISBN 979-8-88644-336-3 (Paperback)
ISBN 979-8-88644-338-7 (Hardcover)
ISBN 979-8-88644-337-0 (Digital)

Copyright © 2023 Mary Elizabeth Browning Fallis
All rights reserved
First Edition

All rights reserved. No part of this publication may be reproduced, distributed, or transmitted in any form or by any means, including photocopying, recording, or other electronic or mechanical methods without the prior written permission of the publisher. For permission requests, solicit the publisher via the address below.

Covenant Books
11661 Hwy 707
Murrells Inlet, SC 29576
www.covenantbooks.com

Beautiful Shades of Love

Mary Elizabeth Browning Fallis

No matter their skin color
Or the color of their hair.

God loves the little children.
Just like He loves His Son.

God made the earth
And every grain of sand.
He made every person
From every land.

He made the colors of the rainbow
And all the shades of man.

Whether you are short or tall
Born in winter or born
In fall.

God made the seasons.
And He made us all.

He made the oceans.
He made the sea.

He made the birds.
He made the bees.

He made it all for
You and me.

So let us love each other
And live this life with fun.

I thank you, Father, Lord of heaven and Earth,
that you have hidden these things
from the wise and understanding and revealed them to

LITTLE CHILDREN

(Matthew 11:25)

Honor all people, love the brotherhood, fear God, honor the king. (1 Peter 2:17)

Before you were formed in the womb, I knew you. (Jeremiah 1:5 NIV)

About the Author

Mary Fallis is a member of AACC (American Association of Christian Counselors), having studied through Light University.

Mary has a love for nature, science, family, and all of God's creation, especially children.

Mary hopes to touch the hearts and minds of children everywhere.

Printed in the USA
CPSIA information can be obtained
at www.ICGtesting.com
LVHW071542220824
788996LV00010B/43